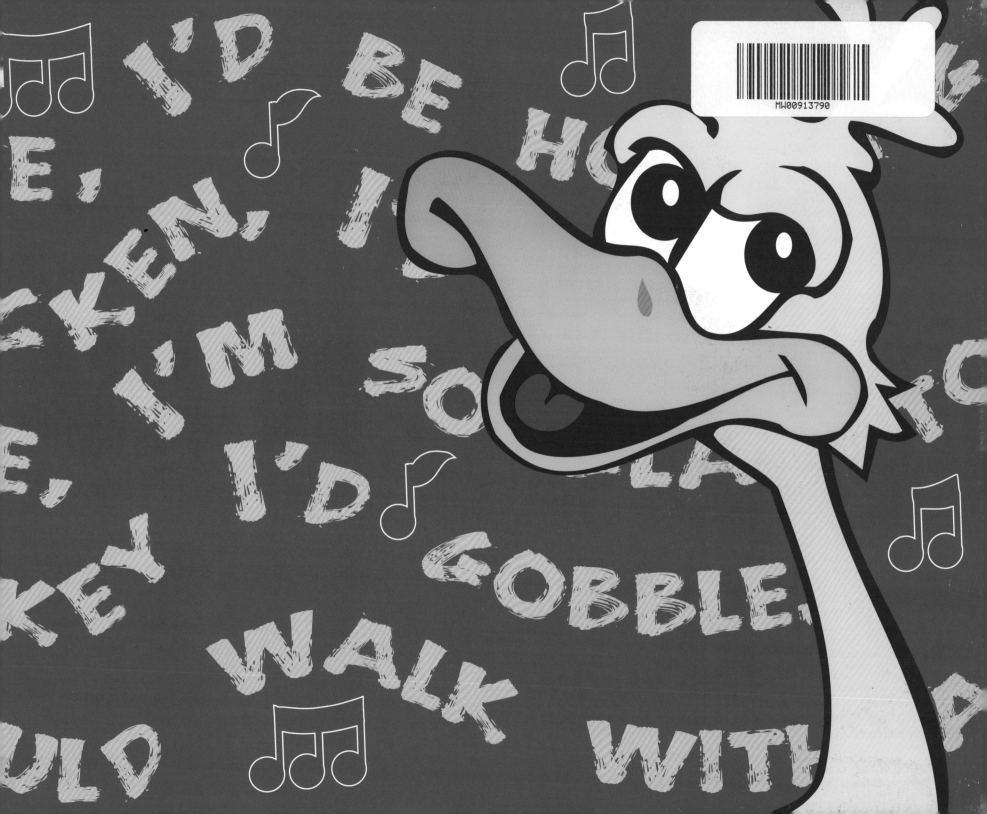

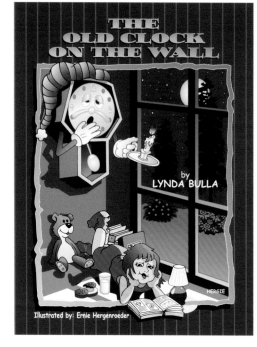

Dont miss these other
exciting books
by:
Lynda Bulla and
Ernie "Hergie" Hergenroeder

The story **"The Churkendoose"** is an imprint of KATY-DID Publishing LLC
Published by KATY-DID Publishing LLC
5845 Eldorado
San Joaquin, CA 93660
Copyright © 2004 Lynda Bulla & Ernie Hergenroeder
San Joaquin, California
Printed in Hong Kong
10 9 8 7 6 5 4 3 2 1

Library of Congress Catalog Number 2003096288
Lynda Bulla & Ernie Hergenroeder
The story of "**The Churkendoose**" written by Lynda Bulla
Illustrated by Ernie "Hergie" Hergenroeder
Edited by: George & Marion Weller
Summary: The Churkendoose, a strange bird that brings harmony to
          this very special barn yard and it's inhabitants.
ISBN:0-9724272-2-8 (Hardcover)

1

THE CHURKENDOOSE

by
LYNDA BULLA

Illustrated by
Ernie **HERGIE** Hergenroeder

II

Once upon a time, in a very special barnyard, there lived lots of chickens and turkeys, ducks and geese.

They were a noisy group, always arguing.

The geese thought they were special and the best fowl in the yard because they had the longest necks and the loudest honks.

The turkeys thought they were best because they had wonderful tail feathers that spread out like a fan, and they were the largest of the birds.

The ducks thought they were best because they had lovely white feathers and could stand on their heads in the water to search for food.

The hens thought they were the best because they laid the most eggs and could scratch the ground for the best bugs, grubs and worms.

2

One day a very strange thing happened and it is still talked about in the barnyard today. *An egg appeared!*

Tom turkey saw it first. *"An egg,"* he said, *"there's an egg on the ground."*

"Why isn't it in a nest like eggs should be?" quacked the duck.

"Who laid this egg?" honked the goose.

"Not I", said the turkey. *"It must be the hen."*

"I didn't" clucked the hen. *"It doesn't even look like a chicken egg. Mine are always in the nest where they belong."*

3

"*Where did it come from?*" asked the turkey.

"*What are we going to do with it?*" asked the goose.

"*Do we want to hatch it?*" *asked* the duck.

Meanwhile, the egg just sat there in the barnyard.

"*It's just an egg and I sit on eggs all day long,* clucked the hen." *Let's hatch it!*

4

"All in favor of hatching, raise your wing," proposed the goose.

The chickens and geese were all in favor.
The turkeys were split, about half in favor and half were
opposed to adopting the egg. Most of the ducks missed
the vote as they were still arguing over where it came from.

"The ayes have it," the goose said.
"Majority rules, we adopt the egg."

"Okay, now what?" asked the turkey, ruffling his feathers.

"Let's get it in out of the cold," said the chicken.

The geese found a string and the chickens made a harness. The chickens and turkeys and geese all pulled together and soon the egg was safely inside the coop. The ducks didn't help because they were mad that they had missed the vote.

6

The chickens were best at sitting on eggs, so they organized a schedule to keep the egg warm.

7

Hours, days and weeks passed; there was no sign of anything happening.
The geese and turkeys were on a daily patrol past the coop.
The ducks tried to ignore the whole thing, but they could be seen whispering among themselves.
Everyone was hoping that there would be news soon.
The tension was mounting, until just when the birds thought they couldn't stand it another minute, there was a tiny wiggle from the egg.

The chicken that was sitting on the egg
felt a gentle movement.
"It's time," she clucked.
*"Quick, everyone, we are soon
to see what we've found."*

The noise in the yard got
very loud indeed.
Geese talked with their loudest
honks, ducks quacked,
turkeys gobbled,
hens clucked, everyone
talking to anyone who
stood near them.

CRACK

A tiny crack appeared;
then a little hole, and
soon two eyes peeked through.

"Hello!"
said the goose, in its most polite voice.
"What kind of bird are you?"

"That's a silly question,"
said the turkey.
"It's not even hatched yet."

10

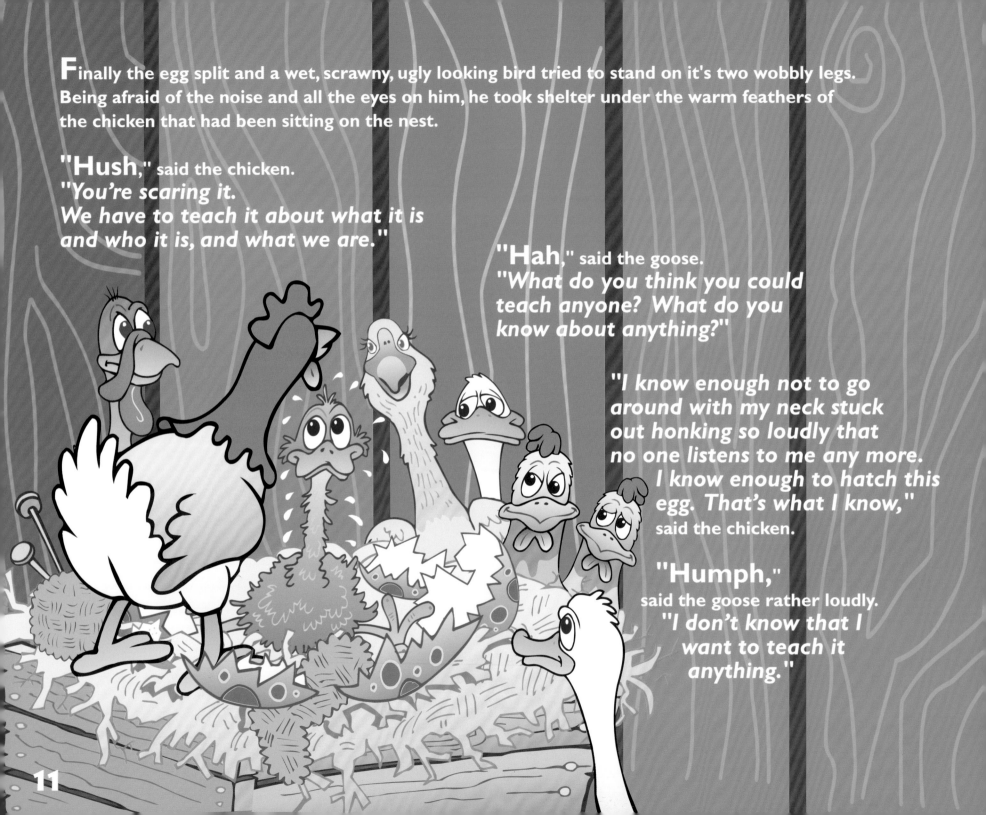

Finally the egg split and a wet, scrawny, ugly looking bird tried to stand on it's two wobbly legs. Being afraid of the noise and all the eyes on him, he took shelter under the warm feathers of the chicken that had been sitting on the nest.

"**Hush**," said the chicken.
"*You're scaring it.*
We have to teach it about what it is
and who it is, and what we are."

"**Hah**," said the goose.
"*What do you think you could*
teach anyone? What do you
know about anything?"

"*I know enough not to go*
around with my neck stuck
out honking so loudly that
no one listens to me any more.
I know enough to hatch this
egg. That's what I know,"
said the chicken.

"**Humph**,"
said the goose rather loudly.
"*I don't know that I*
want to teach it
anything."

11

In a few days the young bird's feathers were a lovely golden brown with just the tiniest bits of white and yellow flecks across it's back.

The chickens wanted to give him a name.

"Why should you be allowed to name him?" asked the goose.

"Because we hatched him," replied the hen.

"But we found him," said the turkeys.

Before the argument got too loud, one young duck stepped onto the nest and said,

"why don't we ask him what he wants to be called?"

"Why should we do that?" asked the turkey.

"If we let him choose, maybe it will help us to know who he is," responded the duck.

"It will never work, but you need to find out for yourselves," said the goose.

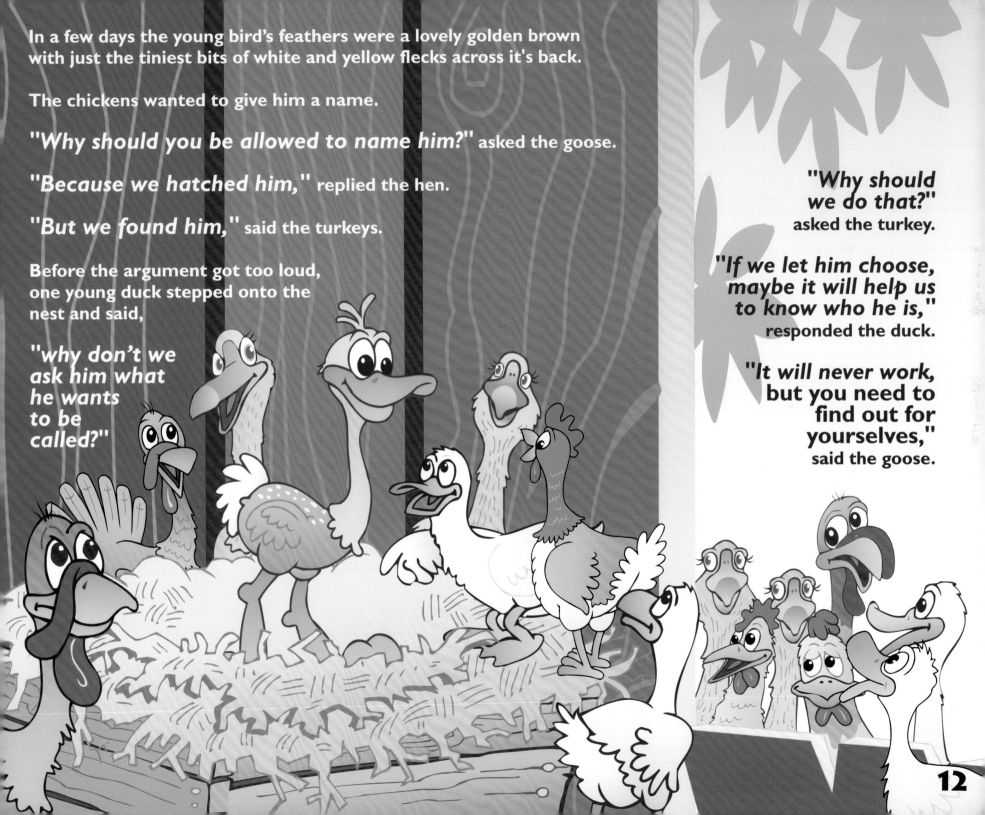

12

The fowl all gathered quickly around the coop.
"*Come here kid,*"
they cried.
"*Come tell us what to call you.*"

The hatchling poked its head out the door and was a bit frightened by the huge crowd gathered around.

"*Call me?*"
he croaked.
"*What do you mean?*"

"*You know, a name,*" said the goose.
"*I'm a goose, the white one's a duck, that's a turkey, and this is a chicken. We all have names. It is part of who we are. So what do we call you?*"

13

The hatchling looked around and said,
"I don't know. I'm brand new.
Do I look like a turkey, a goose,
a duck or a chicken? Maybe I'm
one of you. I really want a name,
now that you say I should have one."

"We are leaving it up to you,"
said the turkey.
"For now we'll call you Sam.
That is neither chicken, turkey,
duck or goose.
It's just a name for you to use."

"Sam, I like it. I'll use it until I pick
a name I think is me, something special."

14

Some of the younger geese went
strutting around the yard with nothing to do
except tease Sam, **"*There he is,*
No name Sam,
No name,
No name,
No name Sam."**

Then they would fall on the ground laughing at their rhyme.
This made Sam feel funny inside, but he didn't say anything about it.

Young Sam spent some time with the chickens
learning how to scratch and dig for grubs.
He learned to fluff his feathers,
but he couldn't cluck.

Sam spent some time with the turkeys. He was learning how to hold his tail up high, though he couldn't spread it into a fan like the older birds could, and he couldn't gobble.

*H*e spent some time with the geese and He learned to hold his neck just so, and strut around the yard. Honking was not for him.

Sam spent some time with the ducks learning to wiggle his tail and waddle. They tried to teach him to swim, but he didn't like that at all.

All the while the young fowl of the yard would tease him and say, *"There he is, No name Sam, No name, No name, No name Sam."*

16

Soon the grownup birds were meeting
and talking about Sam's training and education.
As time passed the arguments became fewer
and there was more cooperation .
They started asking questions and caring
about each other's ideas.

One day Sam was scratching the dirt and
found a particularly fat and wonderful grub.
One of the young turkeys saw Sam's special
way of turning over the dirt.
The youngster got curious and said,
*"That is a truly wonderful grub
you found. Would you show
me how to find them?"*

"Sure," said Sam.
"Come scratch like this."
Soon Sam had all the young
turkeys scratching the dirt
and finding big grubs,
bugs and worms.

Sam was peering over the fence and saw cows and green grass and a silo.
"*What are you looking at?*" asked a young chicken.
"*It's a beautiful land beyond the fence,*" said Sam.
"*I wish I could see,*" said the chicken.
"*Here,*" said Sam., "*climb on my back.*"
And soon all the chickens could see beyond the fence.

The young geese were fascinated by Sam's ability to hold his tail so high.
They thought it added an air of dignity to the young bird.
The young geese, wanting to be very dignified, asked Sam
to teach them to hold their tails high.
And soon all the young geese looked
very dignified indeed.

The young ducks liked to hang around with Sam because he was kind and gentle and he didn't make fun of their wiggling tails and waddling walk.

Sam didn't have a name, and when the young birds were bored, they would gather around him and chant, **"There he is, No name Sam, No name, No name, No name Sam,"** and Sam would have that funny feeling inside.

Sam did have a special talent.
He could sing.
He sang the most beautiful melodies.
The birds would stop to listen when he practiced his music.
The chickens fluffed and clucked with joy.
The turkeys gobbled softly to the beat, and the geese and ducks swelled with pride at Sam's accomplishment.
He was a songbird. The most wonderful of all birds since music brought such joy. They envied his talent.

19

Because he could sing he was treated as an outsider. *Sam asked the elders what he should do.*

"**Y**ou have a beautiful voice. *It's a gift that needs to be shared. We love to hear you sing,*" they said.
"*We all wish we could sing. Instead we only cluck, gobble, quack, and honk.*"

"*But we still need to know who YOU are. You haven't selected a name. You have found a voice, but you haven't found your name. You've brought joy and song into our life but we don't know who or what you are.*"

20

"*I'll think about what I am,*" said Sam.
He began walking and thinking, thinking and walking.
It was very hard work. Slowly an idea
began to form.

Churkendoodles?
Churkendoofus?
Duckenturse?
Turkenduck?
CHURKENDOOSE!

"I'm neither chicken, turkey,
duck nor goose, but they
have taught me all that I
know.
So, I'll be a Churkendoose.
No one else is a Churkendoose."

The Churkendoose song

"If I were a goose, I'd be honking.
If I were a chicken, I'd cluck.
I'd swim with glee, I'm so glad to be me, if I were a duck.
If I were a turkey, I'd gobble.
As a goose I would walk with a strut.
If I were a hen, there'd be eggs in my nest.
I would quack if I were a duck.
I have friends that are happy and helpful.
I have friends that like me so much.
I can be who I am, my name can be Sam, but its not, I can tell you that much.

Refrain:

I'm not chicken or turkey or goose, yet all of them is in me.
Not chicken or turkey or duck or goose.
I am what I've chosen to be.
Not chicken or turkey or duck or goose, a Churkendoose is me.

I like that I have fine brown feathers and a beak that is ever so cute.
A neck that is long while singing a song and a voice like a horn I can toot.
I was raised by the fowl in the barnyard, I was taught to be all I can be.
I have chosen this name, may it live on in fame, the Churkendoose is me.

Refrain

I'm not chicken or turkey or goose, yet all of them is in me.
Not chicken or turkey or duck or goose.
I am what I've chosen to be.
Not chicken or turkey or duck or goose, a Churkendoose is me.
I'll say it again my fine feathered friends, the Churkendoose is me."

23

The Churkendoose story is a true example of what happens when an entire barnyard works together, each doing their special part, all equally important to the fulfillment of the end result. We would be amiss if we didn't acknowledge the following:

Aldene Hergenroeder, Ernie's mother, for planting the concept of the Churkendoose within Ernie in 1946, which made the visual interpretation of this book possible many years later.

Karen Gearhart, for searching the internet and discovering a copy of the original book written by Ben Ross Berenberg.

Lynda Bulla, for finding a copy of the original song performed by Ray Boldger and for taking the challenge upon herself to rewrite the story and song maintaining the concept of people helping people by working together regardless of their differences.

Dan Paisano, of the Good Company Players, for coordinating the production of the Churkendoose song and finding the voice for the Churkendoose.

Kent Hillman, for his superb arrangement, interpretation and performance of the Churkendoose song.

And to the many children who will learn to practice the very concepts that are presented in this little book, and for perpetuating those concepts to future generations.

Lynda Bulla dedicates this book to her granddaughter Amy Paolercio who knows the value of teamwork.

Ernie dedicates this book to his eleven wonderful grandchildren, which are too numerous to picture.